Suggestions for Teache

1. This book is designed to be READ by a teacher o ages 3-11. Some children, about 8 or older, can handle and up should be old enough to read and understand everything in this book, including the "Teacher/Parent Notes" in the back of the book. **Media Specialists:** when checking this book out to Middle School students, point out the supplemental reading in the "Teacher/Parent Notes" section, for enrichment of the text.

2. The section called "Teacher/Parent Notes" in the back of this book is designed to help augment the text of this book. The notes are divided by page applicability, e.g., notes at "Enrichment for page 1" should be read by the teacher/parent before reading the text on page 1 to the child/ren and the information dispensed as you deem appropriate, based on the ages of your audience.

3. Almost all children love to be read to, and shown the pictures from that reading, though not all have the same ability to sit still long enough for the reading of this entire book. Attention spans of children differ, (1)depending on their ages, (2)the time of day/evening the book is read, (3)activities that are planned before or after reading time, and (4)the time the book is read even during the school year (is it daylight or dark outside?). Suggested length of reading times include added discussion time to allow for questions and enrichment.

    a. Ages 3-7 -- 20 minutes.
    b. Ages 8-11 -- 30 minutes.
    c. Ages 12 and up -- the entire book.

4. Plan enrichment activities around a Spring or Fall discussion of "life cycles." In the case of "Flutterbye," she is a fourth generation Monarch butterfly, which means she is born in September, and will start migrating almost immediately, but will still live until around March. Most other books on butterflies would be appropriate for Spring application or "new life" timeframe, since few other butterflies live for the same six months that a fourth-generation Monarch will live.

5. Plan art, science, research, group, or field trip activities around this book, by teaching a unit on butterflies, focusing on:
    a. The importance of insects that pollinate plants.
    b. The differences in plants and their usefulness to an area (Hint: Monarchs like milkweed, which is a toxic weed and is not wanted in most cultivated or planned landscape areas. Without milkweed plants, will you get Monarchs to lay eggs?).
    c. Fragility of insects versus their strengths.
    d. Usefulness of flying insects versus crawling insects (and arachnids) versus burrowing insects.
    e. The beauty and symmetry of butterflies' wings.
    f. Differences in the ways various butterflies use their wings at rest (Hint: most butterflies flap their wings slowly while they rest or eat, whereas most Monarchs leave their wings spread open when they rest, for maximum sun absorption time).
    g. Draw, color, and cut-out butterflies and hang them from a mobile or from various places around the room, for continual viewing. This will provoke questions and discussions during the day.
    h. A series of essays, for older students, discussing butterflies and evolution, psychology, imagery, etc. See the author's books called *The Five Finger Paragraph* series, for more information on implementation of this suggestion.

Flutterbye, the Butterfly

Written by
Johnnie W. Lewis

Illustrated by
Johnnie W. Lewis

Photographs by
Johnnie W. Lewis
and Friends

Marietta, GA USA

The main characters in the book "Flutterbye, the Butterfly"
are Flutterbye and her friends. In her journey to her
"wintering home," Flutterbye's experiences teach her about
herself and and her life.

Lewis, Johnnie W.
        flutterbye, the butterfly/Johnnie W. Lewis

DEDICATION

This book, and all such books by me, are dedicated to the child in all of us, who love nature, who love life, and who love butterflies.

Special thanks go to:

★My Better Half, Jimmy Lewis, for his undying love, support, kindness and paycheck!

★My children, Tash Lewis White and Trevor MacKenzie Lewis. I would never have been inspired to write for children if I had not had you. Thanks for your tolerance of your errant mother!

★My grandchildren, Parker and Avery White. You are the lights in Mammy's eyes. Thanks for being my audience and sounding boards. I love you!

★My dear friend Jan Bernard for the extra pair of eyes!!

★All of my "photographers," especially John Humphreys and Jerry Battle. Your work is impeccable!

★Children everywhere who want to learn about nature in our lives. Learn to chase your dreams as you do butterflies!

Johnnie W. Lewis

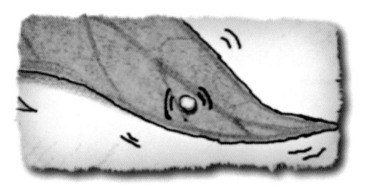

In the early morning dew, as the sunlight warms the egg on the leaf, the animal inside starts to move around, cracking the shell. Ah, now there is more room to stretch. But the egg is so tiny that soon, all that stretching breaks the egg more and more, until the little worm-like caterpillar is out of its first home. The very *first* thing it wants to do is to taste the leaf or branch it is on.

"Crunch, crunch, snnnuuffsnuff, snaarrffsnarf, aarrmm-mmm, this tastes goooodddd, snarf, snarf," the tiny creature says. The little **caterpillar** is about 1/4" long (it could fit across your little fingernail!), but it is much too busy chewing up that leaf to say much else today. And before nighttime, when it will DREAM of eating, it eats 20 more leaves, grows another half an inch longer, and *never* stops eating. All. Day. Long.

Our little caterpillar is an eating machine, the *whole* time it is a caterpillar. Sometimes, it is called a "stomach with legs"!!

There are only two things that our caterpillar needs to worry about. One is how to get to the next leaf to eat it. What do you think the other worry is? That's RIGHT! Something might want to eat our caterpillar!! The best that our caterpillar and its brothers and sisters can do when a **predator** arrives in the area is to hide under a leaf somewhere.

Oh no! There's a red-shouldered hawk that might like to eat our caterpillar! No, it flew away. Must have been looking for a fat mouse instead! But that rattlesnake might want to taste our caterpillar! Do you think that tortoise might be interested in caterpillar casserole for supper? Probably not today. But after the caterpillar becomes a butterfly, they may want to eat it!

With all of that eating and growing, our caterpillar will outgrow its **exoskeleton** very quickly. In other words, it will get "too big for its britches" and will have to change those pants (its skin) several times as it grows up.

Our caterpillar will **molt** about four times before it gets full-sized. That means that its **exoskeleton** will turn hard, crack down the middle of the back, and the caterpillar will break out of that shell, with a newer, softer **exoskeleton**. Which will eventually become too small, harder, and will crack open…

By the time our **caterpillar** gets ready to **molt** the last time, it will be about 1000 times the size it was when it hatched from its egg! It will attach itself, with a strong silk-like thread that it makes in its own body, to a twig, branch or leaf, while its **exoskeleton** becomes a sack for it to go to sleep in.

In this sack, called a **chrysalis**, our caterpillar's body changes into its next stage of life. Now that our **caterpillar** is safely tucked inside its **chrysalis**, something amazing starts to happen. Its body starts falling apart! Really!! Its body turns to a juicy MUSH. But, from that rich MUSH, the tiny little parts rearrange into a form that can fly. In a week or a little longer, our **caterpillar** will become a butterfly!

The day has come! Our caterpillar has been forming inside its **chrysalis** for about ten days now. It is ready to see the world! But some things have changed for our beautiful caterpillar. We know it's a **female** butterfly now, by the coloring on her wings, and she is not going to crawl around anymore. And she can not eat leaves anymore. And she does NOT look like a caterpillar anymore.

We are waiting for our butterfly to get her strength, which usually takes about an hour after she **emerges.** During that time, she will hang around, just like the picture of this Owl Butterfly here which is hanging onto her **chrysalis.** As she hangs there, her blood pumps through her wings, making them straighten out and stretch. Her wings will become almost **rigid** and will remain stiff like that for the rest of her life. She no longer has a mouth. She has a **proboscis**, a long "straw" that she puts into flowers and drinks nectar with. But she can think, even if she doesn't have a mouth..., sort of. And she can wonder about things, just like you!

"Ah. I feel like I've been asleep for a LONG time! Hmmmh, what is this I'm standing on?" she says to herself, as she leaves her **chrysalis** and walks out onto the leaf where it is attached. She scratches with one of her feet, tasting the leaf.

"The first thing I want is something to drink," she thinks as she walks upside down on her leaf. But while she walks, something keeps knocking into her bottom. She has VERY big eyes now and can look onto her back without having to bend backward.

"Oooooh, what are those big things?" she thinks, looking at what's on her back. "I wonder if they move." She climbs to the top of the leaf while she moves the "big things" on her back very slowly at first, watching them as they move. "Cool! These big colorful things move!" She doesn't know yet that she has four of those "things," but she knows that they are there for a reason. The "voice in her head" is her **instinct** and that voice tells her that those "things" are her wings, which will help her fly.

She has two wings up front, near her head, and two further back, closer to her tail. She moves them up and down, back and forth. Once, while moving them, she feels her feet lift off the leaf. "I wonder if these things will help me move around better than I used to move on my feet, when I was a caterpillar."

Slowly she flaps her wings, then more quickly. Her feet are being pulled off her **chrysalis**! Slowly, but surely, as the butterfly waves her wings back and forth, she feels lighter, as if she could FLY! "I wonder if flapping these wings will lift my whole body."

She moves her wings enough that she is lifted off the **chrysalis**, then she lands back again. She tries one more time, this time turning her body and wings over so that her eyes can see the sun and her feet are hanging down. "Oooooh, I feel free! OH, this is WONDERFUL!! I think I'm FLYING!" She flaps her wings hard enough that she flies to a leaf on the next flower. "Ummm, that was hard work," she thinks. "Guess it's time for me to store up some food." She stops. "OH, NO!" she says to herself as she puts one of her feet to where her mouth used to be, "I don't have a MOUTH anymore! I can't EAT! What am I going to do?!? I need FOOD!"

She moves her **antennae** around quickly, sniffing the air, trying to find something to eat.

"Oh, look. I have one of those curly things like THAT thing has," she says, watching another butterfly on the next leaf. Uncurling her own **proboscis**, she carefully sticks it down into the flower and feels..., liquid? What is that stuff? "Oooh, that feels yucky!" she says as she quickly jerks her **proboscis** out of the flower and curls it back up.

But **instinct** tells her to try again. This time, she carefully puts one of her FEET down into the flower, to touch the liquid. "Ah, that tastes good," she says, "Kind of sweet!" Very **gingerly**, she puts her **proboscis** back down into the flower and sucks. "AH! Yes, I'm gonna like this stuff! And it's easier to get than chewing up leaves!" Sweet nectar from flowers, mostly milkweed, is all that she will eat now, for the rest of her life. But, she has to feed all day, just like she did as a caterpillar. All. Day. Long!

Now that her FIRST **priority,** something to eat, is satisfied, our butterfly looks around at her new world. "WOW! These colorful things are everywhere! I wonder if they all have same liquid stuff that I like in them." She tries out her new wings to fly over to another flower. "I'll just plug into this **fragrant** thing and grab some more 'go' juice!" Our butterfly has to sip ALL DAY LONG in order to have enough energy to keep flying.

Another thing she needs to keep flying is sunlight. She needs about 8 hours each day of sitting in the daylight, in order to keep warm enough to fly! Imagine what it's like for her on cloudy days. Do you think she flies very often then? Or what do you think she does when it rains?

"Now," she says as she sips her next meal, "What am I, I wonder?" She really has no clue as to WHAT kind of creature she is. All she knows is that she **vaguely** remembers being a caterpillar, with many feet that were kind of sticky and held her onto a branch or leaf, she chewed on leaves all day long, and she had a long, fat body. So our butterfly has to discover HERSELF as she flies around, sipping her supper soup all day long. She knows she is not a caterpillar any longer, but she's not sure what she really is.

"There are some pretty colors over there. Maybe those colors have tasty liquid stuff for me to sip," she says as she flaps her wings hard and flies in the warm sunshine to the next batch of color.

"I wonder if I am like that thing down there," she thinks as she flies over a field. "That thing has legs and feet like I do. But I think I've got more legs than it does. And it looks bigger and furrier than me. And look! It does not have any wings!"

"Looks like I'm going to have to stop flying for a while. I'm tired," she says as she passes over a large body of water. Actually, it was just a pond, but anything that size must be quite large to a little butterfly!

She pauses long enough to look over the edge of a lily pad and sees something reflected in the water. "That must be me!" she thinks. "That thing in the water has flappers like I do, and 1, 2, 3..., 6 legs, and a drinking straw," she calls her **proboscis**. "I wonder if there are any others like me. I've only seen one other thing like me, the one I watched to learn how to eat. I need to start looking around."

As she sips at the flower on the lily pad, she sees another creature, that almost looks like her, but not quite. "You have four wings and six feet and you can fly. What kind of flier are you?" she asks it.

"I'm a dragonfly, you silly butterfly!" the creature squeaks loudly. "Don't you know what you are? We're different, but we are alike, too. And we do have the same creatures that want to eat us, so be careful out there," the dragonfly buzzes. Our butterfly studies the dragonfly for a while.

"I guess you're right," she says to the dragonfly. "You do have four wings and six legs, like I do, and big eyes, but you really don't look like me," our butterfly admitted. "You look like..., a dragonfly!" she said, flying away.

"That dragonfly is right. I need to be careful. There may be things that want to eat ME!" Now, she starts to worry. It isn't even night time yet, on her first day out of her **chrysalis**, but she has already found out several things. She can fly, she drinks all of her food, she has large orange and black wings with white spots, she is a butterfly, and something out there wants to EAT her! "That's a lot for my little head," she says. "Maybe I need to have a long drink and think about all of this!!"

She flies to the next colorful patch, but it is occupied. And so is the next one. And the next! "Seems that you all have the same idea that I do!" she thinks. "And you all look a little like me, except for your colors. More butterflies!"

"Yes, I am a Gulf Fritillary butterfly," the orange and black one says. Both of the other two say they are Eastern Tiger Swallowtail butterflies, even though they are different colors.

Our butterfly asks, while she is waiting her turn to sip, "What are those other things that fly? Some of them only have two wings and two feet," she says.

"The big ones are birds," they all say, flapping their wings. "And some of them will try to eat you, so WATCH OUT!" they say together. "And the little ones are bees and other things. Some of them will try to STING you, too!" they say, as our butterfly flies away. "And watch out for spiders' webs!! If you get caught in one, you can't get out!" she heard as she flew away.

Flutterbye wonders, "Is EVERYTHING out to 'get me'?"

The next three flowers are occupied, too! But there's a tree behind that Swallowtail butterfly, and there are things that might be waiting to make a meal, or at least a snack, of our butterfly. What do you think would want to eat her?

After much flying and sipping, our butterfly has to find a leaf for the night, so she can rest. The next day, she needs to start planning her flights..., around flying and sipping! And, of course, getting her 8-hour dose of sunlight!

The first place she stops today is a bunch of flowers next to a very large building. A lot of those small, colorful two-legged animals are out in the grass, running around, while she is flying over them, wanting to sip her breakfast. Suddenly, a VERY loud noise comes from the big building! Our butterfly does not have any ears, but she can FEEL the noise in the air with her body, and it pushes her as she lands on the flowers in a box.

"Look, Mrs. White," the little girl says as she passes the flower box. "That's a pretty orange and black butterfly on that flower. See the way it tries to flutter by as it lands?" she points to the butterfly.

"Yes, Avery, that's a Monarch butterfly. And it will be flying toward Mexico or Florida soon, now that it's autumn. Let's go back into the school now, boys and girls," the teacher says as she herds her students into the building.

Our butterfly thinks about what the little girl said.

"Flutter by? Butterfly? What does that mean? Is that what I look like when I fly? Is that my name?" she thinks. "Hmmm. That's not a bad sound. Flutter by. Yes, Flutterbye, that's what I'll call myself. Flutterbye, the Butterfly!" And Flutterbye is hungry again. Of course.

The next morning, Flutterbye meets other Monarch butterflies and they tell her something startling. "We need to fly a long way this month, so we can get to a warmer **climate**," they all told her. "We are going to Mexico! Do you want to fly along with us?"

Flutterbye's **instinct** tells her that she needs to fly to wherever Mexico is, where the other butterflies are headed. "The air today is a little bit cooler than when I came out of my **chrysalis**. And there is not as much warm light as there was on the day that I hatched. Maybe I do need to go with the others."

21

"Flying and sipping," she thinks to herself as she passes over the fields. "What a way to live! Nothing to do but fly and sip all day."

"And don't forget about watching out for the things that want to EAT us," one of the butterflies says. "And the rain, and cold, and nighttime, and the WIND!"

"Guess I haven't been around long enough to learn about all those things," Flutterbye says.

A few days later, Flutterbye flies over a building with furry things beside it. "Hey, isn't that the little girl from that other place? The one who called me a butterfly? Hi, Avery! It's me, Flutterbye!! I'll just flap my wings really hard now and maybe she'll notice me!" But, Avery and her friend Erin don't understand Flutterbye, because they can't speak Butterfly. Avery just rubs the sheep as she watches the butterfly flit around.

Disappointed that her new friend doesn't recognize her, Flutterbye flits over more animals to another flower, unrolls her "drinking straw" and sucks up the delicious nectar.

The "voice in her head" tells Flutterbye that she needs to fly with all of the other butterflies toward warmer weather and longer days. Her **instinct** won't steer her wrong. And she doesn't know HOW she knows where to go, she just knows that she KNOWS!

Flutterbye will see MANY strange sights in North America, while she's flying and sipping. She doesn't know what most of those things ARE, but some of them will provide some entertainment for a while! And give her a chance to meet MANY more fliers like herself, while she hides from OTHER fliers and **predators**! It will take Flutterbye about five to six weeks to get to Mexico or southern California, where she will spend the winter. She and millions of other Monarch butterflies will live out the winter months in that warm weather, until it's time for them all to fly back "home."

One day, Flutterbye sees a lot of white things stacked up together. "OH, that looks like a cool place to land!" She doesn't know that they are elk antlers stacked up to make an arch over the road. But they sure look like a nice place to rest. "Oh, isn't that little girl down there the one I saw before?" she thinks as she flaps her wings at Avery and her brother, Parker. "Oh, she is waving at me this time! Maybe she DOES remember me!" Flutterbye says.

Another day, as the sun is setting, Flutterbye sees something VERY strange! Someone has planted the front ends of cars into the ground, leaving the rear ends pointing up in the air!

"Those 'people boxes' that run so fast on the ground are stuck IN the ground. How silly!" Flutterbye says. But she flaps her wings to wave at her friends, Parker and Avery, who are also there to see the silly sight!

Then, there is the day that Flutterbye takes a wrong turn and flies into a tunnel of some sort. "There has to be a way to get back to the warm light," she says to herself. "Maybe if I turn here. No, looks like maybe it's this way. Uh-uh, maybe it's..., oh wait, Flutterbye, you goofy Butterfly, just look UP and the warm light is up there." She flies out of Antelope Canyon, not wanting to get "stuck" in THERE again! It is cooler in there, but it is darker, too! "And if I can't see THEM and get away, they might try to eat ME!" she thinks.

During her journey, Flutterbye has almost been eaten by a tortoise, two frogs, a rattlesnake, three lizards and salamanders, a heron, a seal, four geese, a cat, and an osprey! The scales that she lost in the battle with that little frog will not grow back, but that won't bother her flying! It was the praying mantis that REALLY scared her! "If I fly too low to the ground, the four-legged animals come after me. If I fly too high, the two-legged ones with wings want to eat me! It's time for this journey to END!"

28

And it does. At the end of thirty-four days, Flutterbye and her flying companions arrive at the "trees" that they have all been talking about. There are Monarch Butterflies EVERYWHERE! "I'm not sure if we will find a place to land and rest, much less find something to eat, Monty!" Flutterbye sputters. Monty is her butterfly friend who has been flying with the group of butterflies. He's a **male** Monarch and he has black patches on his hind wings that she does not have.

They have never SEEN so many other butterflies like themselves! But their **odyssey** is over, for now, and there will be plenty of time for them to rest and eat and relax, all through the winter months from October to March.

During the whole winter, Flutterbye, Monty, and their friends spend everyday doing the same things. They wake up, look for a flower with nectar, fly around collecting heat from the "warm light," as Flutterbye calls the sunshine, and resting.

By the middle of February, most of their friends are getting restless and wanting to fly away "home," wherever home is for them. Flutterbye's **instinct** tells her that she can't fly too long each day, because it's not really warm yet where she needs to go. The butterflies need food along the way. They need places to rest when they're tired. So much to think about! OH, and watch out for **predators**!

But there is another driving force in Flutterbye's very near future. She knows it's almost time for her to fly no longer. "The other Monarchs were talking about that on The Tree. Looks like my time is almost over," she thinks to herself. "But I need to do one important thing first. I'm not even sure how that happens, but I think that 'voice in my head' will tell me what to do, when I need to know."

The elk and the moose may have noticed her as she flies toward "home," but they can't speak Butterfly to her. Do you think it would be safe for Flutterbye to rest on one of their antlers for a little while?

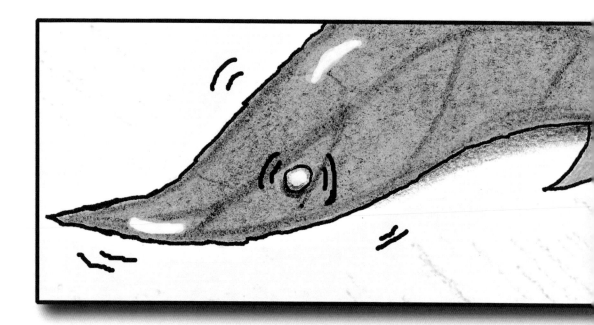

One day, after flying and sipping and resting and flying for hours, Flutterbye and her life partner, Monty, arrive at a big, open field, with a small lake. There are even a few flowers growing in the field. "That's milkweed, my favorite plant!" she says as she spots one down below.

She is so excited about finding the RIGHT place to lay her eggs, that she and Monty do a special "dance" in the air, fluttering around each other in spirals, like they are dancing in the air. They dance for a long time, until they are tired. Flutterbye needs nectar. Monty flies to the edge of the pond and sits, almost in the muddy place, drinking the muddy looking water for a long time.

The next day, Flutterbye very carefully lays her eggs, one on each plant leaf so that the caterpillars born from each egg will have plenty of food to eat as soon as they hatch.

She won't be there by the time they hatch, but she knows that she's left an "**instinct** voice" for them to be guided by, a voice that will tell them how to act, what to eat, where to fly, and what **predators** to watch out for. She's leaving a "mother's voice" to teach them.

Flutterbye has completed her **circle of life**.

Ten days later, in the early morning dew, as the sunlight warms the egg on the leaf, the animal inside starts to move around, cracking the shell.

And a new Flutterbye is born…

GLOSSARY

antennae -- *noun* \an-ˈte-nə\ a pair of long, slender movable segmented sensory organs on the head of insects, myriapods, and crustaceans.

caterpillar -- *noun, often attributive* \ˈka-tə(r)-ˌpi-lər\ : a small creature that is like a worm, but with many legs and that changes to become a butterfly or moth.

chrysalis -- *noun, often attributive* \ˈka-tə(r)-ˌpi-lər\: the sack in which a small, worm-like caterpillar with many legs changes to become a butterfly or moth.

climate -- *noun* \ˈklī-mət\ : a region with particular weather patterns or conditions; the usual weather conditions in a particular place or region.

circle of life -- *noun;* biology : also called the "cycle of life," it is the series of stages through which a living thing passes from the beginning of its life until its death.

emerges -- *intransitive verb* \i-ˈmərj\ : to rise or appear from a hidden or unknown place or condition : to come out into view.

exoskeleton -- *noun* \ˌek-sō-ˈske-lə-tən\ : an external supportive covering of an animal (as an arthropod).

female -- *noun* \ˈfē-ˌmāl\: an individual that produces eggs or young; a girl or a woman.

fragrant -- *adjective* \ˈfrā-grənt\: having a pleasant and usually sweet smell.

gingerly -- *adjective* \ˈjin-jər-lē\: very cautious or careful.

instinct -- *noun* \ˈin-ˌstiŋ(k)t\: a way of behaving, thinking, or feeling that is not learned : a natural desire or tendency that makes you want to act in a particular way; something you know without learning it or thinking about it; a natural ability.

male -- *noun* \ˈmāl\: a man or a boy; a male person; a male animal.

molt -- *verb* \ˈmōlt\biology : to lose a covering of hair, feathers, skin, etc., and replace it with new growth in the same place.

odyssey -- *noun* \ˈä-də-sē\: a long journey full of adventures; a series of experiences from which someone learns knowledge or understanding.

predator -- *noun* \ˈpre-də-tər, -ˌtȯr\: an animal that lives by killing and eating other animals; an animal that preys on other animals.

priority -- *noun* \prī-ˈȯr-ə-tē, -ˈär-\: something that is more important than other things and that needs to be done or dealt with first.

proboscis -- *noun* \prə-ˈbä-səs, -ˈbäs-kəs\biology : the long, thin nose of some animals (such as an elephant); a long, thin tube that forms part of the mouth of some insects (such as a butterfly).

rigid -- *adjective* \ˈri-jəd\: not able to be bent easily.

vaguely -- *adjective* \ˈvāg\: not clear in meaning; stated in a way that is general and not specific; not thinking or expressing your thoughts clearly or precisely.

TEACHER/PARENT NOTES
(only those pages requiring additional "enhancement" will have Enrichment Notes)

Enrichment for page 1

Depending on the species, the caterpillar (or larval stage of a butterfly or moth), can eat for as long as 18-20 hours a day. Several caterpillars together can eat every leaf on a plant the size of a bush within a few days. Caterpillars are not worms. Worms do not have feet, but all caterpillars do, whether they are the larval stage of butterflies or moths.

It is hard to distinguish moth caterpillars from butterfly caterpillars, though they produce completely different creatures after their chrysalis or cocoon (or pupa) stage. Moths, for the most part, are small, have dark, muted colors and fly only at night. They have furry or feathery antennae, and have thick, fur-covered bodies and legs. The beautiful Luna moth is an exception to these generalities.

Butterflies, on the other hand, come in innumerable color combinations, ranging from blacks and browns to blues, reds, oranges, yellows and whites. They have long, thin antennae with a "ball" on the end, called a "clubbed" antenna. Their bodies are usually slimmer with a segmented thorax through which they breathe and sperm is planted in the female, and their legs are usually slender and hairless.

==========================

Enrichment for page 2

The only thing our caterpillar has to worry about other than food, during her whole life as a caterpillar, is something else eating her. She is on the menu for almost all large birds, frogs, lizards, some snakes, and maybe even a moose or a human!

==========================

Enrichment for page 3

Every year, Monarch caterpillars and butterflies follow the same pattern. Three generations of the butterflies will stay in the Northern Hemisphere, usually the USA. The fourth generation of Monarch Butterflies, born in September and October of every year, will fly south and west to very warm climates, in Florida, Mexico or southern California, for the winter months. Both sexes will fly back to the same areas that their own great-grandparents lived to mate and lay their eggs. Theoretically. There's no proof of their return to the same areas, but most scientists believe they do.

What IS a fact is that, every year, the Monarchs return to the same trees in Florida, Mexico and California to winter. If those trees are not there anymore,

Enrichment for page 3 (cont.)
they have to adapt or die, usually the latter. The problem with the butterflies returning to the same areas is that humans are clearing out, clear-cutting, and getting rid of more butterfly habitats every day, decreasing areas for the butterflies to eat, live, and breed.

A Monarch Butterfly lays her eggs, usually one to a leaf, so the emerging caterpillar will have food as soon as it hatches. She will only lay eggs on milkweed plants, and since that is a prolifically growing weed, her caterpillars will always have plenty of milkweed plants to eat. Unless there are no milkweed plants.
==========================

Enrichment for page 4
Monarch Caterpillars have a tough exoskeleton, which they will "molt" several times during their short lifetimes (usually only about a week to ten days in length). Their last molting will produce a sack that they will hang in while their bodies completely liquify and the molecules rearrange to form the butterfly. This sack is called a chrysalis. The process of metamorphosis IS called the "cocooning process," but the sack for a butterfly is called a chrysalis. A cocoon is made of silken threads, made by a worm or moth caterpillar, for its pupa stage.
==========================

Enrichment for page 5
Although the chrysalises (or chrysalides) shown are for the owl butterfly from Malaysia, this is representative of how numerous "butterflies in waiting" would look. This picture was taken at the Cecil B. Day Butterfly Center at Callaway Gardens, in Pine Mountain, Georgia. The butterflies at that facility are imported in chrysalis form from other countries with tropical regions.

The USDA requires that the butterflies produced from the chrysalides shown NEVER interact with native species in the United States. The butterflies produced from these chrysalides will live and die in that solarium, so they can't compete with the native butterflies for food and space. In fact, the USDA will impose a fine of $25,000 for any butterfly that is allowed to "leave" the facility, whether accidentally or by "theft."
==========================

Enrichment for page 6
Few caterpillars resemble the butterfly they become. But the fact that a worm-like creature like a caterpillar shuts itself up into a small sack and its body liquifies to become a completely different creature is nothing short of a miracle!
==========================

Enrichment for page 7
Butterflies don't have mothers around to tell them what to do, so a newly emerged butterfly has to rely on instinct to tell it right from wrong, how to fly, when to land, where not to go, things to watch out for, etc. If her instinct is wrong or she doesn't follow what her instinct tells her to do, she could be dead very quickly!

Most creatures on Earth, except for some mammals (such as humans, dolphins, apes, dogs and cats), do not have brains that "think," yet they function very well by following their "instinct." Instinct is believed to be an imprinting on the DNA of the animal (even mammals have instinct), which are instructions for the animal to follow in almost every situation. This instinct is what leads male butterflies to drink muddy water or fourth generation Monarchs to fly toward the setting sun or warmer climate each year in the Autumn, when looking for their winter resting place.
===========================

Enrichment for page 8
This page is total speculation on what the author thinks might go through the butterfly's mind, if it could think, on its first trip to drink after coming out of its chrysalis. Shock, followed by speculation, followed by experimentation.

Obviously, butterflies don't talk, but putting the narrator's voice into our butterfly will make it more of a "discovery" adventure for younger readers.

Butterflies will hang around on or near their chrysalises for up to an hour before they attempt their first flight. Kind of like a baby bird attempting its first flight, a butterfly is a little scared the first time, since flying is something that it has NEVER done in its LIFE, up to this point!
===========================

Enrichment for page 9
Smelling with her antennae and tasting with her feet for the first time must feel VERY strange to a butterfly. The same strangeness would go for drinking through a "straw" for the first time, instead of eating!

===========================
Enrichment for page 10
A butterfly's lifespan is tenuous, at best. Most butterflies will live for a maximum of 6-8 weeks, in all of their four stages -- egg (1 week to 10 days), larva (caterpillar - 10 days), pupa (chrysalis - 1 week to 10 days), and adult (butterfly - 2 to 6 weeks). If the ambient temperature is low or there is not much sunlight for days on end, these conditions could very easily hamper a butterfly's ability to stay alive.

Enrichment for page 10 (cont.)

Butterflies, just like caterpillars, usually hide on the underside of a leaf when it rains. They also try to hide there when danger lurks or flies over.

===========================

Enrichment for page 11

Smelling with their antennae and tasting with their feet are very different ways of using their "senses" than humans use them. Try using your own feet to "taste" your hamburger or use your hair to "smell" the air! The butterfly is trying "new things" with her brand new senses.

===========================

Enrichment for page 13

A few facts that are common to all butterflies. Dispense this information as you see fit. Butterflies:

Weigh less than most flowers
Can fly, as the Monarch does, for sometimes thousands of miles on its journey
Have compound eyes, like all insects
Smell with their antennae
Taste with their feet
Use their proboscis, which measures up to an inch and curls under, to feed on
       plant nectar
Are cold-blooded
Need eight hours of sunlight to stay warm enough to fly
Spend most of the day eating, like caterpillars do

===========================

Enrichment for page 14

Butterflies have been called that for THOUSANDS of years. The ancient Greeks recognized the creatures in some of their literary works, so we know that butterflies existed back in ancient times. But it wasn't until the Middle Ages in Europe that we find any reference to the name of "butterfly" for the creature. The creatures were seen to land on newly churned butter, apparently "tasting" its sweetness, hence the name "butterfly."

Charles Darwin was even quoted in his book "On the Origin of Species" about the number of "flutter-bys" on the islands of Great Britain. Whether or not the creatures were, at that time, called flutter-bys and the name was mutated to butterflies, or vice versa, is not known and is pure speculation. What do you think? To me, the author of this book, the name "flutter by" makes more sense than butterfly as the name for the creature, since that's what it DOES, it flutters by as it flies!

===========================

Enrichment for page 15
Obviously, we may never know if butterflies experience fear. Their natural timidity comes from their instinct, which tells them to be wary of things they aren't sure of or that are bigger than they are.
==========================

Enrichment for page 16
Different species of butterflies do not normally congregate on the same plant, as each species is "attracted" to different plants. But stranger things have been known to happen!

The Eastern Tiger Swallowtail Butterfly is the state butterfly of Georgia, the author's home state!
==========================

Enrichment for page 17
For the most part, the predators of butterflies are reptiles -- frogs, lizards, some snakes -- and spiders. Yes, spiders! Web-spinning spiders usually sit at the edge of their web, waiting for a flying insect of any sort to get caught in its web. The spider then hurries to the ensnared insect to wrap it completely in more webbing. Once the encasement of the creature is complete, regardless of the size of the insect, the spider feeds on the creature's blood.

Not all flying things eat butterflies, because the coloring of a butterfly is USUALLY an indicator to the predator of toxicity of the butterfly. But some birds, frogs, and lizards will try!
==========================

Enrichment for page 18
Consider a class project. Let your student(s) draw pictures of the animals that might try to eat butterflies.
==========================

Enrichment for page 19
Some Monarchs will fly a very long way and need to get started on their journeys by September or October.
==========================

Enrichment for page 20, 21
Monarch butterflies are the "most recognized" butterflies in the world, probably because they have four generations per year. There are always three generations that live in whatever locality you might find them in the USA, Canada, and northern Mexico. The first generation emerges from the egg about 4 days after it is laid in March/April. The caterpillar eats, grows, and lives on milkweed plants for about two weeks before it creates its chrysalis and begins its metamorphosis. After ten days, the chrysalis opens and a new butterfly

Enrichment for page 20, 21 (cont.)

emerges, which will live for two to six weeks before it lays eggs and dies. This process is repeated with egg laying of the second generation in May/June and the third generation in July/August.

But the fourth generation lives from its chrysalis emergence in September/ October to fly up to 2,500 miles to Florida, Mexico or southern California, depending on how close the destination is to where he/she was hatched, so it can live through the winter months in a much warmer climate. After six to eight months in the warmer climate, in February/March, the Monarchs will return to wherever they came from (theoretically) before mating, laying their eggs, and dying. Then the first of the yearly generations of the Monarchs begin again.

Obviously, butterflies don't talk, but putting the narrator's voice into our butterfly will make it more of a "discovery" adventure for younger readers.

==========================

Enrichment for page 22, 23

Occasionally, during flight or when resting, a butterfly will encounter an "obstacle" which may cause damage to a wing. The butterfly can STILL fly, if the damage is not too great. If the wing is broken or broken off, usually the butterfly will die. But if some of the scales that cover the wing, providing lift and color to the wing, are damaged or removed, or the wing sustains a small hole, the butterfly can usually still fly. The damages cannot be repaired. In fact, MOST of the Monarch butterflies that reach their destinations in Florida, Mexico, or southern California, will have some wing damage.

==========================

Enrichment for page 24

You may never see many butterflies flying together, until it's time for the annual "migration" to Florida, the southwestern United States and Mexico. For a few weeks in September and October, Monarchs by the HUNDREDS fly over all of the southern states to get to their warm wintering places. Imagine the sights they see during their flights!

Technically, Monarch butterflies don't have predators, since they are toxic to most animals that try to eat them. But, as with Flutterbye not KNOWING how to fly and what to eat when she first left the chrysalis, very young animals of ANY species might TRY to eat Monarchs before they find out that they should NOT try to eat them! THOSE are the predators about which Flutterbye needs to worry!

==========================

Enrichment for page 25

The "arch" of elk antlers shown on this page is located in Jackson Hole, Wyoming. Every year, the Boy Scouts of America and other youth groups gather elk and moose antlers in the area to sell, raising funds for their own troops and

Enrichment for page 25 (cont.)

groups. The leftover antlers that are not sold MAY wind up in the arch! Imagine a lot of butterflies stopping to rest on the arch!

===========================

Enrichment for page 26

The "Cadillac Ranch" is a silly, crazy, but FUN tourist attraction located on Route 66 outside of Amarillo, Texas. Begun in 1974 by hippies from San Francisco and their silent partner billionaire Stanley Marsh III, this "modern art" was erected to show off the evolution of the Cadillac tail fins, from the 1949 Club Sedan to the 1963 Sedan de Ville. All of the Cadillacs face west in a straight line and have been in the ground longer than they were on the road. The public is encouraged to visit the free exhibition. Just bring your can of spray paint and a camera!

===========================

Enrichment for page 27

It is only BARELY possible that Monarch butterflies would come to Antelope Canyon, since it's located in a desert, but you never know! The author's grandchildren visited the area, took pictures, and wondered if butterflies might visit the canyon.

Antelope Canyon, the most visited and most-photographed slot canyon in the American Southwest, is located on Navajo land near Page, Arizona. From above, the canyon looks like a wide crack in the sandstone. But, down inside the crack, are beautiful walls carved completely by water over millions of years. The system of canyons has been opened to the public, by permit only, since 1997, when the Navajo Nation turned it into a Navajo Tribal Park. Photography within the canyons is difficult due to the limited amount of sunlight which filters down from the top, usually only between March 15th and October 7th each year. The Canyon System is closed when a lot of rain falls 7 miles upstream, as that will cause serious flash floods in the lower canyons.

===========================

Enrichment for page 28

Although many Monarchs are killed by innumerable types of animals, few are actually eaten. The Monarch has those bright colors for a very good reason -- as a warning because it can be toxic to some predators when eaten! Maybe the reason they are toxic/poisonous to predators is because they eat the poisonous milkweed plant as caterpillars. There is even a "false Monarch" butterfly, called a Viceroy, that looks VERY much like a Monarch, but is not toxic to a predator. This imitator is usually safe from predators because potential predators are warned off by the same bright colors of the Monarch.

The colors on a butterfly's wings are actually a collection of scales, overlapping and layered on the butterfly's wings like the shingles on a roof. The butterfly can still fly when missing some scales in small areas, or even with a hole in a wing.

Enrichment for page 28 (cont.)

But flying with a large piece missing from a wing would make survival for the butterfly very hard.

==========================

Enrichment for page 29

As was stated earlier, the fourth generation of Monarchs travel sometimes great distances to overwinter in Florida, Mexico and southern California. Imagine what effect such long journeys have on their wings and bodies. Some arrive at their destinations with parts of their wings missing. All they are after then is nectar and a warm place to stay for the winter.

==========================

Enrichment for page 30

Overwintering in Mexico may sound like fun, but the trip back "home" is long and arduous. This trip usually begins for the Monarchs in February, even though their final destinations may not be warm yet. Those locations usually are warm by the time the Monarchs arrive in March to mate and lay their eggs.

==========================

Enrichment for page 32

Mating and death, though sensitive subjects for smaller children, are part of the Circle of Life of a butterfly. For that reason, those subjects are included in this narrative, though "glossed over," for you, the adult, to dispense to your child/ren audience as you deem appropriate for their age and maturity.

Male Monarchs have small black patches on their hind wings in which their sperm are carried. The sperm is deposited in the female's abdomen once the two butterflies arrive at their destination. Because of the severe loss of fluids extracted from the male's body during this "operation," male butterflies, of most species, will fly to muddy waters to replace the fluids and sodium lost during copulation. Male Monarchs live for a few days after this operation, but female Monarchs die shortly after laying their last eggs, usually within a couple of days.

==========================

Acknowledgements

The following people were kind enough to submit their own photographs for this book. No photographs have been included from public websites without permission. All illustrations are by Johnnie W. Lewis.

Sherrie Blanton Adams: page 24 (alligator)
Patricia Ferguson Allen: page 16 (right)
Jerry Battle: pages 2 (left and center), 17 (heron and osprey), 18 (center), 24 (geese and Luna moth), 28 (heron and osprey)
Jim Boland: page 17 (pelican)
Rhonda Edge Brock: page 28 (cat)
Danny Crooks: page 24 (hummingbirds)
Brooke Rowland Erwin: page 24 (swallowtail butterfly)
Allison Howard Photography: pages 14, 28 (yellow frog)
John Humphreys: pages 5, 15 (center and right), 16 (center), 17 (hornet and bee), 18 (left)
Sandi's (Spires Nobles) Photography: pages 6, 7, 8, 9, 10, 15 (left), 17 (cardinals), 19, 20 (right)
Pam Gilchrist: page 18
Suzan Hugues-Kennedy: page 28 (praying mantis and brown lizard)
Johnnie W. Lewis: pages 1, 3, 4, 11, 13, 20 (left), 28 (tortoise and geese), 32, 33, and cover artwork
Julia Sallee Ligosh: page 24 (brown moth)
Edna McGlamory: page 16
Donna Mock: page 17 (spider web)
Cynthia Noyes: page 28 (frog on screen)
Sharon Woodard Oliver: page 24 (the peacock)
Julie Jackson Peele: page 23
Mandy Schreiner: page 28 (green chameleon)
Linda Scott: page 17 (praying mantis)
Laphon Smith: pages 24 (dragonfly on toe), 28 (salamander)
Jade Summers: page 28 (rattlesnake)
Tash Lewis White: pages 2 (right), 12, 25, 26, 27, 31
Alissa Wright Wilkerson: page 17 (baby duck)
Edda Tucker Patterson: pages 17 (raven), 24 (kitten), 28 (seal), 34

Thanks, Danny, for the "circle of life."

Thanks, Jimmy, for the "bye."

Look for other books by the same author, Johnnie W. Lewis, available on Amazon.com:

The Five Finger Paragraph series (grades K-12)
The Writing Police series (grades 2-6)
The Five Finger Essay (grades 9-12)

And future books by Johnnie W Lewis:

Flutterbye's Flying Friends

Made in the USA
Charleston, SC
08 March 2015